ROAD TRIP TO DEVIL'S TOWER

(And other stories)

By

Allen L. Scarbrough

It all seems kind of stupid now.

I had just signed the divorce papers in late June of 2002 that ended my six year marriage and hungered to do something extraordinary, as much to convince myself I was still alive as to prove to my ex that I was a man of consequence. When my ex heard of this adventure she laughed out loud.

"That's the most ridiculous lark I've ever heard of and proof positive I was married to an ass," she said to her mother, who nodded.

I would drive across the states of Oregon, Utah and Wyoming and back in six glorious days in my 1973 Pinto and redefine my life and my purpose, maybe even see God. However, my big mistake was telling someone about it. The sad story is I have a big mouth. After concocting my brilliant plan I skipped off to Skeeter's house, as he was a world leading authority on Pintos and my good friend since our days at the Albany Daily

Republican. Skeeter had operated the press, that is, until he broke it. Skeeter lived in a singlewide trailer, known to all as the metal mansion, with a fat tub of goo named Bubba Lewis.

That fateful night I was sitting alone in my one bedroom shit hole apartment pouring over a map of the United States when I hopped up to go to Skeeter's and get a new water pump for my Pinto. I needed my car more than ever since it would have to haul my carcass across the three thousand miles of the trip. It was high time to fix the pump that had been acting up for several years. A single malfunction of the vehicle could strand me on some lonesome desert backwater, buzzard meat or worse. There is nothing like the thought of horrific death to motivate a man like me. So off I went, a small cloud of blue smoke trailing behind me as onlookers said to themselves, what the hell?

I passed the end of Albany and headed straight for Tangent, a dinky town in the middle of the Willamette Valley that had once been the grass seed capital of the world. I passed Buck and Betty's diner (a wonderful dive that served great homemade chili that gave me green diarrhea) and turned onto Fourth Street toward Skeeter's metal mansion. Skeeter was out in the shed cleaning some car part and I could see him working furious and forlorn through the open door. Skeeter was a good man and never let his semi-illiteracy stop him from achieving great things in the automotive world. Skeeter was a well-respected authority on cheap and discontinued automobiles. For all my misguided education I could not repair a 1973 Pinto if God himself had given me personal directions.

"Skeeter, you old fart," I said hopping out of the Pinto and hitting the gravel drive, "What've you been up to?" Skeeter came out of the shed wiping a cylinder with a rag. He smiled when he saw me and halfway put his arm around my shoulders.

"Nothin' much shithead," Skeeter said, referring to me by my affectionate nickname. He motioned me into the house and I followed.

Inside the odorous house, shelter being the better word, the ubiquitous Bubba sat in a wide recliner eating a bowl of cheese-whirl's while watching Oprah. Bubba was unemployed forever. His mother had died and left him life insurance that generated the sum of fifteen thousand dollars a year, enough for Bubba to pay half the rent, fuel up his pick-up with its oversized tires, and feed himself into a coma each and every night. Skeeter loved his friend Bubba, but I only tolerated him.

"Hey Lee, what's new?" Bubba asked chomping down on a cheese-whirl.

"Nothing much. I quit my job and now I'm going to take a trip to Devil's Tower," I answered, sure to send shock waves through the room.

"Oh," Bubba replied. However, Skeeter's eyes glazed over and the wheels of his limited imagination turned.

"Wowzers old buddy, that's a pretty fur piece of travelin'," Skeeter stated.

"Three thousand miles or so all together. Should be the trip of a lifetime," I replied.

"Well you've got the best car in the world for long distances. A Pinto will get you there ever' time," Skeeter stated with authority. I thought for a moment and considered what he had just implied. A Pinto will get you there every time? The words made no sense to me. It was as if God had made a new commandment and then spoke it in backwards Aramaic.

"Skeeter, my Pinto doesn't even get me to the store every time," I responded.

"That's because you don't know your vehicle," Skeeter said, "What you need on this trip is an expert. Like me for instance."

I had to admit he had a point. An onsite mechanic just might come in handy. And though it was Skeeter Heaves I was talking about he would at least be able to make some conversation. I might have to listen to tedious diatribes on professional wrestling and mind numbing discourses on the virtues of Pintos, but at least Skeeter would be a warm body to travel with, and he could help with gas.

"Why don't you come with me Skeet?" I asked, "It'd be fun to have a traveling buddy." Now this was a colossal lie, but it was a hard subject to broach, that of just wanting him along in case of a breakdown. In truth, if I had owned a new car I would never have asked, but I was about to travel the breadth of the western United States. The devil would not drive to hell in a 1973 Pinto.

Skeeter's head danced in an array of half willed extravaganzas. Visions of Ontario, Salt Lake City and outer Wyoming waltzed through his skull and landed with a thud.

"You mean it? I can go. You know old buddy I've wanted to see Wyoming since I was a little boy. I can't believe it's coming true. Oh my Lordy," Skeeter blasted with his tongue, "Skeeter Heaves about to see the west."

"All right now Skeet, don't get too excited. We're not leaving until the week after Fourth of July. And you're paying half the gas," I stated with no exceptions allowed.

"That's all right Lee. I need some time to get that kind of money together anyways. I'll have to sell some things," Skeeter said already putting together an inventory of Pinto parts that he could sell in a few days. Bubba, who had been listening half to us and half to Oprah, chimed in his exalted opinion.

"I think you two are full of shit if you think you can get all the way to Wyoming on what you two have for money. Skeeter hasn't worked in six months and ran out of unemployment yesterday, and you Lee, never have more than a few bucks no matter how much you make, and to think you have a college education."

It was hard to stand there and be brow beaten by a fat tub of goo, but he had a point. Money would be needed and Skeeter and I had little of it. Not that Bubba was rich, but he did get a check every month from his mother's estate. I steadied myself for the inevitable.

"Hey Bubba, why don't you come along too? We'll just make it a great big road trip we'll never forget," I said wishing I could kill the Bubba before having to ever be in a car with him for three thousand miles. Why is necessity the mother of all vexation?

"Oh I'd love to come along Lee, just love to," Bubba replied with glee. It was not so much that he wanted to come that bothered me, but that he wanted to come so much he would spend all of his mother's check. This meant I would be his bitch for the longest six days of my life. I began to have second thoughts. I remembered something my father used to say, 'never invite a girl to a dance you wouldn't take home to mother'. I doubted that it meant anything, but it was what swam through the murkiness.

"Great. We're leaving the Sunday after the Fourth of July so make sure you two are ready. Skeet, I'll swing the Pinto by before we leave for a look see and Bubba you get a list of food items together to fill the cooler. I'll take care of the travel itinerary."

Neither of the two understood the word itinerary, but they assumed it was something a college boy like me could handle. I might own a shitty car and be broke from my divorce from the hoary beast of death (Cindy, as her parents called her), but I was a smart son of a bitch and Bubba and Skeeter knew it. Hell, even my Pinto knew it.

The next few days passed without incident. I plotted the course of our journey using a straight edge and a mile guide and calculated that we would need to average five hundred miles a day to make it all the way to Wyoming and back in the six days I had allotted. I needed to look for work and since I would be broke upon return six days was all I could afford. Besides, one more day than that and I was sure I would murder Bubba and Skeeter and leave their bodies on the side of some backwater road in Wyoming where even buzzards feared to tread. It all seemed so certain of success. I basked in the glow of victory before taking the field. I was a gambler, a rambler and a man with a boob and a bulge in the car. I was on my way to glory. I would see Wyoming by God.

Two days prior to leaving I rambled out to Skeeter's to get the Pinto looked over. It had been running fine and except for the light blue smoke fuming out of the tailpipe, a few missing lights and a broken windshield, it ran like a top. The battery was suspicious, but I had no money to replace it so I ignored it. I have always wondered, however, how someone ever came up with the particular shade of yellow my Pinto sported, had there been a contest and this color won by default? Was it the product of several colorblind buffoons? It did not seem to me that human beings had created it. To me it had come from another world where horrid colors were glorified. My friends referred to it as that kinda yella color.

I pulled into Skeeter's gravel drive and parked behind Bubba's gigantic pick up. A big black lab jumped up on me as I started for the back door and I picked up a stick and threw it far and he ran off after it, surprised upon return when he found me missing. I had slipped into the brown and white home that reeked of bacon grease, dead rodents and pine-sol. Skeeter came out of the bedroom having just awakened at noon and greeted me with a smile and an offer of coffee.

"You're out and about awful early," Skeeter stated pouring grounds into an ancient coffee maker.

"Skeet, it's noon, early was five hours ago," I replied, "I want you to look the Pinto over and see if it's ready for the road."

"Oh it's ready. A Pinto is always ready," Skeeter said with bemused assurance.

I never knew where his love of Pinto's came from except that he was the best in the world at fixing them and so had a vested interest in promoting their worth. I thought they were horrible, a small step up from a

Gremlin. I owned a Pinto for one reason and one reason only, my ex wife wanted me to have one.

"Still you need to look it over, see if I need to do anything before we leave. Three thousand miles is a long ways from home," I stated with paternal authority.

"Sure thing shithead," Skeeter replied filling a pot with milky colored liquid that oozed from the tap. I heard a thunder coming from the back of the home and knew that Bubba had stirred. Bubba Lewis was one of those human beings that had never worked for anything in his life, but seemed to get along just fine. He was happy in a depraved, deluded kind of way. Happiness is just getting what you want out of life. If you want very little, happiness is indeed possible. For those of us that dream of bigger things we are sure to reap disappointment by and by.

"I thought I heard something," Bubba stated, plopping into a dining table chair that hated his guts.

"Just out to get Skeet to look over the Pinto," I said, "Don't want a breakdown crossing the plains of Wyoming."

"There are airplanes in Wyoming?" Bubba asked.

"Yes Bubba, there are planes in Wyoming." I responded just to keep the boy happy, after all he was the finance minister of our expedition. Bubba would pay any price to come on my adventure. If I had to put up with inane chatter from Tangent to Kalamazoo it would be worth it, or so I thought at the time.

"Let me put on some clothes and take a look at the Pinto," Skeeter said.

"Sure thing Skeet, here's the keys," I said tossing the keys high into the air.

"Be right back," Skeeter said disappearing around the corner.

"I can't wait Lee. This is so exciting. I'm about to wet my pants," Bubba stated. I prayed to God he would not.

"Should be a hoot Bub, a real trip for the ages."

"You think we'll get to see Verbooht. I hear you can smell sausage for miles and miles," Bubba said drifting into hot vibrant arias of misappropriate indulgences.

"If it's important to you Bub we'll make it a priority," I replied cementing the deal for perpetuity.

"You mean it Lee, you really mean it?" Bubba asked, eager and excited.

"I promise Bub."

Just then Skeeter danced around the corner dressed in a coffee stained bathrobe, a pair of tattered boxers and a pair of mismatched cowboy boots. He exited the metal mansion, no comment necessary.

Out the window I could see Skeeter working his magic. Though it was almost impossible to get a 1973 Pinto to run Skeeter could make the machine purr like a kitten. He had a gift. It was as if the Pinto understood Skeeter as much as Skeeter understood the Pinto. It was zen-like, quantum mechanical and plain weird. I heard a supple vortexian noise emanate from under the hood. A few tweaks of this and that and the Pinto had never sounded better. Even the blue smoke turned a new shade of purple. I sat and admired the genius of my friend. Machines loved him, though no woman ever had.

The Sunday after the Fourth of July arrived with only one minor catastrophe. Bubba had held a bottle rocket too long and burned his hand, but nothing would stop him from making my life miserable for the next six days. He could have lost both legs and still gone on my trip. And it was my trip. It was my plan, my vision, my 1973 puke yellow Pinto. I had sold the

wedding ring my ex dumped on me to roust up enough cash to at least pay

the gas. I hated that I needed the likes of Bubba Lewis to pay for food and

entertainment, but life loves to toy with our dreams. I had the whole six

days planned to a tasty tee. First a drive to Salt Lake City through the

backwaters of Oregon then on through Wyoming to the Devil's Tower and

back home. Oh how glorious my sweet supple mind, how marvelous the

works of my hands.

I packed the Pinto and was on the road to Skeeter's by eight o'clock.

To make Salt Lake City would take thirteen hours give or take, not

accounting for the loss of an hour due to Mountain Time. I knew Bubba

would be at the back door, bag in hand, but Skeeter might take a few swift

kicks in the ass to get going. The day was glorious, the summer sun

dazzling in its multitudinous rays. I felt like the first explorers must have

felt, full of lust and hunger. I needed breakfast. I arrived at the metal

mansion pondering the infinite, loving life and staring at the neighbor's

wife in the front window with her robe loose to her waist. Bubba charged

the car and stood at the side door like a golden retriever with a tennis ball

in its mouth.

"Hey Lee," Bubba said, a smile branded to his mouth, "Skeeter's not quite ready, but can I put my stuff in your car?"

"Sure Bub, put it in the back," I replied as disinterested as a whore at a nudist colony.

"Great. I can't wait to get this party started."

I hopped out of the Pinto and rushed through the back door disappearing like a wisp of cloud on a dry day. Skeeter was nowhere to be found.

"Skeet, where in the hell are you?" I shouted through the putrid palace. No response. I crept down the long hallway to the back bedroom and discovered Skeeter Melvin Heaves kneeling before the porcelain prince. I was flabbergasted, on the first day of my exalted trip to Wyoming Skeeter had gotten plastered. I wanted to yank his testicles with a weed puller and toss them out the window.

"Oh, hey shithead. I had a little too much to drink last night, sorry man," Skeeter said with tan debris on the outer edge of his thin lips. He stumbled to an upright position and exposed his genitalia to my eyes. I would rather have seen a chubby chick in a thong.

"Skeet, for Christ's sake get some underwear on," I replied with a wrinkle on my face, "You know I don't want to see that."

Skeeter looked down at his miniscule tinker and flushed red.

"Oh shit. I better get something on," Skeeter said before rattling over to the dresser and taking out a thread bare pair of cotton briefs, "It's really cold in here you know."

"Skeet, it's July," I replied and the subject was dropped.

It took some doing, but before long I had Bubba and Skeeter in my Pinto along with all their crap and camping gear and a fine breakfast of strawberry pop-tarts at my side. Skeeter looked almost human in jeans and a t-shirt with the obnoxious saying 'I erupted on Mount St. Helens' on the faded green front. Bubba liked the back seat and that was fine by me, but I have to say he looked quit handsome in his slacks, work boots and dress shirt two sizes too small. Wardrobe to Bubba meant whatever was on deep clearance.

"Let's fire this baby up and hit the road!" I squealed with arrogant affirmation.

"Let's get Lee. I want to see me Wyoming," Skeeter said, still dazed by his hangover, but coming to life at last. Skeeter put on some sunglasses he had found along the highway to Tangent and looked like a movie star with his chiseled features. If Skeeter had had a brain he just might have been a star. But why, I thought, had that not stopped any of the others?

"Oh my lord god Jesus," Bubba exclaimed, "I'm going to miss Oprah for a whole week, not to mention Gilligan's Island."

"Life is about sacrifice Bubba. Somehow life will compensate you for your enormous loss," I replied thinking up homilies faster than a firefly in heat.

"I hope so Lee. It's just more than I can bear right now," Bubba said as Skeeter flicked matches at his head, "Stop that or I'll fart." Skeeter ceased and desisted.

Thinking Bubba might change his mind and thereby leave Skeeter and I hungry I raced the engine and peeled out of the driveway. I fled the town of Tangent, population three hundred people, six hundred turkeys, a few sheep and goats, and stormed toward Highway 34. The Pinto strained under the weight of three grown men, but welcomed the challenge. I peered out the cracked windshield at the vibrant Cascade Mountains and prayed the Pinto would not fall short there. I decided not to tell Bubba and Skeeter

I had failed to include the spare tire and jack. Too much information for a beautiful July day.

We passed the town of Lebanon and dusted up the highway toward the summit of the Cascade Mountains, glorious and compelling. The Pinto belched, farted and struggled to lift seven hundred pounds of humanity to the high places of earth. I was proud of my diminutive chariot. It might be the most god awful color ever created and a piece of shit no self respecting individual would drive, but it drove in heaping, leaping fits and bounds and looked like a sterling alien craft from a dysfunctional planet.

To think there had been a day, perhaps a beautiful July day, when grown and educated men had surrounded a design table and unveiled to the world the concept of the Pinto. How excited they were, how full of achievement and exaltation at all their hands and brains had made and when it was all done a glistening Pinto rolled off the assembly line for all the world to see and then came the collective groan when the full understanding hit them that they had just built a complete and utter failure of mechanical design and color. Chimpanzees could have built a better car using sticks and banana peels. Imagine for a moment the disappointment of their mothers.

"My son builds automobiles for a living," one mother would say, "Oh, what cars?" Another would answer. "I'd rather not say," would come the helpless reply.

Bubba began to get restless and demanded a potty break.

"Bub, there's no place to pull over," I insisted, "Maybe when we get to Sisters."

"Lee I'm not shitting you. I need to pee or I'll go all over the upholstery."

Now the upholstery was a pale tan and well worn with many tears and tatters, but it was my car and I was not going to smell Bubba piss all the way to the far ends of Wyoming. So I pulled over near a tree and pointed. Bubba frowned, but relinquished his dignity and his morning coffee behind a Douglas fir that might never have recovered from the experience. I have never felt so sorry for the Bubba as I did at the moment yellow liquid splashed on his Mighty Mite work boots. I pointed the Pinto toward Bend and we three splendid warriors found grace and beauty in the eyes of the world.

We entered Bend near noon and Skeeter's belly growled as it had since we passed Mount Jefferson and the front of it reminded Skeeter of a big pile of french fries. Bubba's bowels chimed in chorus and the decision was made to enter the domain of the nourished and slaked. I wanted to stop at the diner on the highway known for its magnificent sandwiches, but got overruled when Bubba and Skeeter both eyeballed the Hawaiian Tropical Burger Hut on the south side of the main drag. Just the thought of tropical burgers made my head ache, but I could not deter the two lumps of humanity I had in my car because I was both a technological and financial challenge. Perhaps my ex was right. I was a dreamer and a buffoon, but I was damn good at pretending not to be.

Bubba's eyes grew as he eyed the menu. This was one of those old-fashioned burger palaces that had car speakers and waitresses on roller skates. I rolled down the window.

Bubba shouted, "I want a Hawaiian burger, extra onions, cheesy fries and a chocolate shake."

"Bub, I have to press the button before they can hear you," I replied, wanting to bust out laughing, but stopped when I saw Skeeter's lips about to spout his own order.

"Oh," Bubba replied.

"Okay, everyone know what they want?" I asked.

"Yeah," came the synchronous reply as we tallied our order.

"Here we go," I stated and then pushed the little black button.

"Hello, welcome to Hawaiian Tropical Burgers. What can I get ya?" A shrill, somewhat hoarse, voice responded as if contained in the little metal box in the shape of a clown head.

"Three Hawaiian burgers, extra onions, three cheesy fries, one chocolate, one vanilla and one root beer shake, and that's all," I ordered.

"Okay, that's three onion rings, a Hawaiian burger."

"No, no, no," I replied and repeated the taxing order. We waited for a reply that never came. Circus music spewed from the loudspeaker and Skeeter began to play an imaginary organ. The sun shone overhead like a ball-turret furnace and sweat dribbled off Bubba's forehead in deep autumnal rivulets. Bubba wiped the sweat with a napkin he later put to his mouth.

"It's hot back here Lee, can you turn the air conditioning on?" Bubba asked.

"Bubba this is a 1973 Pinto. We're lucky it has a heater and a key," I responded.

"Pinto's have excellent ventilation shithead. Here let me fix this up," Skeeter replied. Skeeter reached into the glove box, hit something twice and a fan kicked on somewhere under the dash as hot air blasted about our heads.

"See, a little imagination is all it takes," Skeeter stated. Very little imagination, I thought.

We waited and waited some more. Just as Bubba was about to lose it a waitress in a skimpy skirt, tight top and high heeled white roller skates exited the multi-colored building carrying a large tray above her shoulder like a skilled professional. My mouth watered as the smell of fresh fries lilted through the air and into my nostrils.

"Hot damn," Skeeter belted, "And I'm not talking about the fries."

The skinny, flat chested waitress placed the tray onto my awaiting window and demanded the sum of fourteen dollars and fifty cents. I turned to Bubba and he handed me a twenty. The girl handed me twenty-one fifty in change. Counting change is not the strong suit of the younger generation, known as generation Y, as in why did we have these idiot kids?

"That's no….," Bubba started to say before I gave him the look. The girl swam away pushing side to side in a breathtaking and repugnant remembrance of bygone eras. I passed out the food like a benevolent father and the three of us opened our mouths and bit into our Hawaiian burgers with masochistic gusto.

"Oh my god!" Exclaimed Skeeter Melvin Heaves, son of Buttermilk Heaves of the Thoughthollow, Oregon Heaves. As he spoke an unutterable flavor reached my cerebral cortex and lodged forever in my neurons. Rancid pineapple mixed with overcooked onions and meat paste. I almost puked.

"This is pretty good," Bubba said licking some pineapple off his lips.

"Bubba, cow dung and horse ass would taste better than this," Skeeter replied in an exacted replication of the god-awful truth.

"How do you know Skeet?" Bubba replied, his feelings hurt.

"Believe me I know. Hey Lee, get on that squawk box and tell that skinny chick to get her cute ass back out here."

"You got it Skeet," I replied, about to do just that anyway. I pushed on the black button and a clown voice responded.

"Red Clown Burger Hut is now closed, our hours are 11 a.m. to 12 midnight, seven days a week."

"It's noon," I screamed back at the clown box, now chuckling. I looked into the windows of the building and all the lights were out and the door locked. I looked across the street at Granny's Diner, loaded with customers, to see if the power had gone out and a large contingent of satisfied customers seemed to be enjoying their lunch. That's when I noticed we were the only customers at a burger joint on Main Street in the middle of the day. All in all, a bad sign.

"This is a delicious shake," Bubba stated. I thought for a moment that maybe only the burger was bad and at least we could salvage the free meal by downing the fries and shakes. Wrong, dead wrong. I tasted the fries and they had been fried in rotten grease once used for fatty bacon and the shake had rancid pineapple mixed into the frosty concoction. Everything in the place had been made Hawaiian by the addition of rancid pineapple. Savory, Bubba thought.

"This is the worst hell hole I've ever eaten in," Skeeter stated, and that included Buck and Betty's diner.

"Amen brother," I replied tossing the frosty beverage all over the clown's face and shoving fries into its non-existent mouth, "Eat that you useless misuse of metal!"

"Stop wasting food Lee," Bubba exclaimed from the back seat, "I paid for all this."

"Bub, she gave us back more change than we gave her. We made a small profit," I answered the mathematical mastermind in the ripped and ridden back seat.

"Give it to me, I'll eat it," Bubba said, reaching for the shake between the seat. Skeeter and I handed over the remains and Bubba ate to his heart's content. I tossed the tray like a square Frisbee and fired up the Pinto for round two of our glorious adventure of exuberant wistfulness and the potent Pinto responded like a down syndrome Ferrari as I commanded it out of the stall and back into the forbidding and forlorn landscape of eastern Oregon. God how lucky we are, I thought, to live in such a brown and lifeless desert of a state.

After many merciless hours we rambled into Salt Lake City as the lights of the New Jerusalem bounded from their hubs and lit the night sky in eloquent affirmations of God's eternal plan, or so the Mormons say. Skeeter, long faced and beat from the day's journey and the lack of adequate food blathered in inaudible syllables as we passed the great temple on our way to the Holiday Inn on South Temple Street where I had secured a reservation with an over limit credit card. Bubba stared up at the granite monument and was dumbfounded, if indeed it is possible for a moron to be dumbfounded. He was awed by the colossal structure that claimed among many other things to be the habitation of the divine. It looked like a stone building to me, but they say I lack a certain gift of imagination.

"Wow Lee," Bubba effused, "I didn't know Mormons owned Salt Lake City."

"Always have Bub," I replied, "Hell, Brigham Young came through that pass right up there and said 'this is the right place'."

"For what?" Skeeter asked.

"For Zion," I replied.

"Aren't they a rock group from the 70's?" Skeeter asked.

"No," I replied, "Zion is literally, where the righteous dwell."

Skeeter took notice of a prostitute plying her wares on South Temple and said, "I bet she's righteous."

"Well there's been some changes," I replied ducking the Pinto into the parking lot of the Holiday Inn.

The freckled girl at the counter put us in a room on the bottom floor where throughout the night a three-legged polka took place above our heads. Bubba snored so loud I dreamed of being in the battle of Gettysburg as a cannoneer. Skeeter, as usual, slept like a baby in the full realization of perfect thoughtlessness. I awoke often and stared at the ceiling. How had it all come to this, I moaned, to eternal damnation on this fiery hell of a planet? What evil had I committed in another life or on another sphere that had placed me in a Holiday Inn in the middle of Salt Lake City with two dinkuses with an eighth grade education between them? Was I in fact evil, Satan in the guise of a bookstore geek? If I truly was in a heaven on earth, as the inhabitants of the Wasatch Range are fond of preaching, then why was I so alone? Was God dead? Sleeping? Recovering in rehab? O God where art thou, I asked to the air, just as Bubba fumigated the room with a gaseous death cloud from the tropical burger stand. I wept.

In the morning the sun bled through the thin curtains and penetrated the darkest regions of my medulla oblongata. Bubba awoke and dashed into the bathroom for his morning constitutional, which ended up making the bathroom uninhabitable for the better part of an hour. Skeeter and I hopped over to the breakfast room for our free breakfast that had cost us $89.99.

Skeeter loved the little tarts, perky and punctual on their tiny trays. He had

four until the attendant/executioner stared him down on the fifth. I feasted

on stale corn flakes and cold toast until at last obtaining some epicurean

satisfaction by imbibing croissants and butter. Skeeter laughed at the

croissants that he called 'them girly buns'.

Bubba entered the room and smiled. He had put on his tan trousers,

work boots and a gigantic t-shirt that read 'help yourself'. I pretended not

to know him.

"Hey Lee, Skeet," Bubba said as he waddled up to the front of the

line and the floorboards cried for mercy, "Some smorgasbord aye."

"Very tasty," Skeet replied staring into his bowl of fruit loopies.

I sipped coffee and pretended to be at a café in Paris. Skeeter, in his

ripped jeans and cowboy shirt looked on his way to Wyoming for a

roundup. I looked at my two companions and begged for a quick and

painless death. It was just then that 'she' glided in on legs that reached to

heaven, a tall, buxom blonde with a toothy grin and a decided lack of

sense. All three of us followed her backside as it meandered through the

maze of offerings at the counter and when she realized there were no

available seats, save the one next to me, I offered her a chair at the table of champions. She looked us over three times before consenting. Sighing, she plopped into the semi-padded seat and pulled her long locks back over her ears.

"Good morning," Skeeter said in his most polite voice, "Lovely day isn't it."

Skeeter sounded like he was reading out of an English translation manual for Japanese immigrants.

"Yes, it is," she replied sending shivers up my spine. Her voice had the cadence and purity of a well-rehearsed instrument and her eyes shone with the brilliance of a thousand screaming suns, and her breasts were huge.

"I'm Lee Dalwig and my compatriots are Skeeter Heaves and Bubba Lewis," I stated with suave compunction.

"I'm Mandy Monroe. My friends just call me Mandy from Sandy," Mandy opined as milk shot up her nostrils and over her filtrum, "Sorry, I giggle a lot." None of us cared because she also wiggled when she giggled. Bubba stared at the poor girl with the raw eyes of a virgin about to unveil his first conquest. Bubba Lewis had never been with a woman, except the vinyl one he kept hidden from Skeeter in the back of his closet, and longed more than anything to taste the delicate delights of female flesh. Told once that it felt like warm pudding he acquired a rabid taste for the treat, a strange fetish that had always baffled Skeeter.

"Well Mandy from Sandy, what brings you to the big city?" I asked making conversation because I was the only one who could.

"I'm on my way to Boston. I have a part in a play," Mandy stated as though she were a grand actress about to play Ophelia on the great stages of Europe.

"Oh," I said, "What play are you in?"

"I play a witch in the Salem witch trials reenactment at the Wicca Center for the Performing Arts."

"The what?" Bubba asked.

"Bub," I replied, "You know, the Salem witch trials from the 1600's where they convicted women of witchcraft though it was all just a ploy by some young girls for attention."

"Huh," Bubba said.

"Never mind Bub, I'll explain later," I said and returned my attention to the delicious morsel to my left.

"Hey, you know what, we're going that way too. Maybe we'll see ya along the way," Skeeter said excited as a Catholic schoolboy about to see Jesus.

"I might not get there," Mandy said, doe-eyed and innocent, though I doubted she was innocent of anything worth doing.

"Why's that?" Bubba asked, thinking she might be dying of cancer and not live until she made it to the east coast, or so I assumed since I never knew what that man was thinking.

"I don't have a ride," Mandy said with the saddest voice God ever gave to a woman.

"Golly Molly," Skeeter shrieked, "We're going as far as Wyoming and we have an open seat."

"It's Mandy," she replied.

I winced. The putrid Pinto had almost died going over the Cascades with three hunks of humanity. How was the beast going to survive with four going over the Rockies? It would take all of Skeeter's vast knowledge and skill to pull it off. Despite that I agreed to tender a formal invitation.

"If you can help pay for gas we do have an open seat. It's in an old Pinto, but Skeeter here is the world's leading authority on Pintos and he'll get us there," I stated. Mandy looked at Skeeter with newfound admiration.

"You fix Pintos?" She quizzed, "I love Pintos. My grandfather drove one back in the 40's. I think they're so cool."

Skeeter, face flushed to a purple redness, could not bring himself to correct the decade challenged lady.

"Yea, they're a special car all right," Skeeter replied. Boy, he was not kidding.

Mandy pulled out a wallet stuffed with twenty-dollar bills and handed me several of the crisp bills.

"Here Lee, will this help with gas?" Mandy asked batting her long lashes in my direction for the first time.

"Absolutely," I replied, eyes aglow with visions of the handsome Andrew Jackson.

"Then when do we leave?" Mandy asked, her luscious eyeballs spinning in circular exclamations of dizzying aspiration.

"Soon as Bubba gets his fill," I replied, "That might be awhile."

I had trouble with the idea of a young lady deciding on a whim to take a cross-country road trip with three strange men, but it was her dime and her time. Mandy had an agenda. Perhaps she had a disease too. Had all this been random, or had miss Mandy selected us out of a crowd as the likeliest hombres to take her to her dreams? One thing was for sure, she liked Skeeter. I appeared to have no chance and Bubba never had a chance. For whatever reason the beautiful blonde had taken a shine to one of the dimmest bulbs on the planet. I liked her moxie. It took courage to look into the jaded eyes of Skeeter Heaves and see potential.

After a fifth helping of corn flakes Bubba pushed his bowl away and rose up from the chair and belched. It was time to roll. Skeeter brought three duffle bags of Mandy's toward the stuffed Pinto and somehow we managed to fit all the gear and butts into the available seats. The Pinto had the look of a jalopy crossing the Rockies on the way to the Promised Land of the west; only we were headed east and knew there was something there before we left. The Pinto strained under the bulk, but huffed and puffed along the back highway looking for the Interstate and its highflying asphalt that would cart us over the mountains to lands unknown. We all noticed that Utah was a bit like the Mohave Desert.

"Are you sure Lee, that this here Brigham Young said this was the right place?" Skeeter asked, "I mean it's a little more like hell than heaven."

"Yea, I'm sure Skeet," I replied, "He had some imagination, I'll give him that."

"That must have took some set of balls," Bubba spouted, "To tell a whole bunch of people that had just crossed the Rockies that their new home was a desert."

"He had a vision," Mandy chimed, "It came to him in a dream."

"More like a nightmare," Skeeter replied.

"I learned about it in primary class," Mandy said, "I used to be a Mormon."

"Why aren't you one now?" I asked.

"I got excommunicated for an incident with the football team," Mandy stated.

"You played football?" Bubba asked.

"No, I played with football players," Mandy replied and that was the end of that.

The Pinto hummed and the day grew hot as we approached the border of Wyoming and the long stretch of road that led to the far corner where cows outnumbered people and farms outnumbered cars. Bubba started singing television theme songs out of boredom and soon we all chimed in on some of the old favorites, an intellectual journey this was not. We crossed into Wyoming and saw nothing but tumbleweeds and tractors trailers for a hundred miles. Little did we know we had seen the best of Wyoming.

Bubba moved to the front seat after a pit stop to let the two enamored yahoos, Skeeter and Mandy, look deep into each others eyes in search of something that was not in all likelihood there. We humans are always looking for the perfect mate, the perfect companion to live out our perilous days at our side, but the truth is that there is no perfect mate, just millions of candidates. Skeeter eyed Mandy and Mandy eyed Skeeter and I wanted to puke. What did she see in him, I wondered, he's a jackass at least and a doofus in all probability? Perhaps Mandy had not seen my good side and had made a terrible error in judgment. Perhaps I was not as good looking as I thought. Perhaps chartreuse chimpanzees would fly out of Bubba's ass and explain it all to me. A tumbleweed crossed the windshield and blinded me for a moment. I decided the view had not changed all that much.

"Look," Bubba exclaimed after a hot afternoon of driving through nothingness, "There's the road to Devil's Tower. I saw it in a movie once. We gotta turn here Lee, we gotta turn."

There was no possibility of calming Bubba's mind. He was going to Devil's Tower to see aliens, or God, or maybe his doppelganger. It was in my mind just a giant rock formation, but to Bubba it was the place where aliens would first contact earthlings at their leisure. To Bubba there was a potent mystery just around every corner. This is what happens when you watch too much television and eat too many cheese snacks. I imagined the aliens saying the following.

"See that big rock over there Blayling Five?" Clorthing Six would say.

"Yup, big alright."

"Let's strafe the place and make it a Mecca for tourists and numskulls."

"Roger that, Clorthing Six."

"Imagine the press we'll receive. We'll be famous, only the government will deny our existence."

"I say we nuke the White House Clorthing Six."

"Blayling Five you are a rascal, but no, we need the buffoon that lives there to keep our great secret."

"I see your point old friend."

Bubba counted the miles and forced us to eat fried chicken in the car to save time. Mandy licked the grease off of Skeeter's fingers and that's when we knew we had lost our friend to the far side of relationship hell. Skeeter had never had a girlfriend, just a few five minute stands, but things were looking his way since sun-up. God help me though, I could not figure out why. Skeeter had been free of the wiles of women and therefore a likable loser. Once Mandy got her claws in he was sure to turn into a boring purveyor of purity. A nice act if a man can pull it off.

Hours later we pulled into the Devil's Tower National Monument to discover a gift shop at the base of it. Bubba almost ran out of the car in search of candy bars and soda. Skeeter and Mandy hopped out and ran off into the campground in search of whatever and I went over to the base of the tower and stared up at its strange configuration. It was huge, I mean big. It covered the whole of the sky and melted into the air as if dropped in the distant past by a colossal blimp. Amazing, I said to no one, as a spongy white cloud drifted over the top and appeared to take away knowledge and truth from the glorious rock being. Bubba came scurrying out of the store excited as a school marm getting her first look at a naked man.

"Lee, you gotta come see all the stuff in there," Bubba said, exhaling and inhaling with much distress. Bubba was one of those men who could stand at the foot of a glorious work of nature and not see it.

"In a minute Bub, can't you see I'm looking at this incredible rock," I replied, irritated.

"Okay Lee, but hurry in when you can," Bubba said, "I'm going back in and look at all the alien things."

"Sure Bub, go for it."

About that time I became curious to see what my two comrades were up to. I walked through the campground searching high and low for the two spontaneous lovebirds. I was sure that Skeeter was in over his head and might try or promise anything to the blonde beauty he had just met. Men are the most humble after being rejected by females, but far too bold when in the throes of passionate lust, however misguided and foolish. I walked through endless rows of tents and RV's, campers and dawdlers, children with DVD players on their laps enjoying nature and grandmas soaking up the wisdom of yet another game of Rummy. I spied a tent trailer out of the corner of my eye that was rocking back and forth in a curious way. I saw Skeeter's unmistakable cap hanging on the doorknob. Skeeter's bright green and yellow cap that read 'I love my tractor' could be seen for half a mile in the dark. Curiosity overcame me and I approached the flailing metal cabin with fear and trepidation. I stood at the door and listened.

"Oh Skeeter, oh God, oh Skeeter," Mandy yelped from the back of the trailer. What the hell, I thought, whose trailer was this and why was Skeeter risking arrest to be with a girl who had done in half the offensive line at her school. I decided to knock. The trailer came to a screeching stop.

"Oh shit Skeeter, the owner came back," Mandy said making various rustling noises.

"Just a damn minute. It's probably nothing," Skeeter replied and opened the door in tattered boxers, "Lee, what are you doing here buddy? Can't you see I'm busy?"

"Skeet, what the hell are you doing? This isn't your trailer, you could be arrested," I implored. I had visions of scandal swimming in my head.

"No worries man. The owner said we could use the trailer while he went to the top of the rock."

"That can't be true," I responded. Just then Mandy came up behind Skeeter in a t-shirt I had never seen before.

"It's true Lee. I swear to Heavenly Father," Mandy stated using the Mormon synonym for the Almighty. She looked like a fallen angel standing so adorable and cute in the doorway.

"If you say so," I said, "I'll leave you two be, but make sure you're back at the car in an hour or less."

"Bye," Skeeter said slamming the thin metal door shut. I walked back to the car and remembered poor Bubba alone amid millions of available products for sale to suckers at exorbitant prices. Most people feel that the perfect use of nature is to employ it as a base of operations to fleece the public. I entered the gift shop and encountered the largest array of useless merchandise in the known world. I picked up a penknife with a picture of the rock on it and decided to buy it. Bubba saw me and came up to me sporting a pair of binoculars around his neck.

"Look Lee, a pair of binoculars with super vision," Bubba exclaimed with glee. I thought it should have said no buying this piece of crap without supervision. Bubba handed me the glasses and I pointed them at the counter girl with the long nose and a hanging booger the size of a small mountain.

"I see what you mean Bub. You going to buy them?" I asked.

"Already did Lee. Twenty-five per cent off, who can pass up a deal like that?"

Me, for one.

"Let's go outside and wait for Mandy and Skeet," I said starting for the wide doors that led to the best view of the tower. I put the penknife in my pocket and forgot to pay for it. A minor oversight. I stood on the ground outside the entrance to the campground and looked up at the tower through the wonder of super vision and saw two small bodies walking on the top. I got an idea, never a good thing.

"Bub, let's walk to the top of the tower without Skeet," I pleaded.

"Lee it's high up and it looks like a hard trail," Bubba replied, a worrisome grin on his broad, white face.

"Let's just check it out Bub, no harm in that."

"Okay." Bubba looked down at his feet and kicked a small rock. I could tell he was as excited about the hike as a death row prisoner is to see gallows gleaming in the twilight.

We rambled to the start of the upward trail and read the instructions with acute interest. The trail was marked 'difficult' with a man standing with his hands on his hips. I thought better of the trial run and convinced Bubba of the wisdom of staying on flat terra firma.

"You know Bub, I don't think we have time to reach the top before Skeet comes back and there's really no reason to start if you can't finish," I spouted.

"That's what I've been saying Lee. Why start?" Bubba replied, relieved.

"Okay then let's go back and wait for the two lovebirds."

"Lovebirds?" Bubba queried.

"You know, Skeeter and Mandy," I responded.

"Oh, them."

Bubba and I returned to the Pinto and relaxed our bodies on the side of the doors waiting for our two horny compatriots to return. I tried to drain my mind of all thoughts and Bubba did the same, although that required almost no effort. It had been a good ride so far, although Mandy was a bit of a surprise and the fact she had an instant thing for Skeeter was almost a miracle. No matter how hard we try to plan the sun gets in our way. It is always that round sphere of heat that changes everything. We cannot control our destiny because the damn sun lights up a new path at every turn. I like to blame the sun for all my troubles, whoever blamed the moon for a damn thing.

"You know Bub, the light from the sun takes eight minutes to reach us even at the speed of light," I said in an educational tone.

"Why so long," Bubba replied fondling his field glasses as if they were a woman's breasts.

"So long? Why that light has to travel 93,000,000 miles Bub, that's quite a ways," I replied.

"Oh, the sun doesn't look that far away Lee. It's just right there," Bub said pointing to the sky where the early evening sun lay just above the cloud addled horizon.

"It just looks close because it's so big," I stated, getting edgier and more irritated.

"It's the same size as the moon and we landed there," Bubba said putting his field glasses up to his bulging eyes and scanning the territory for alien craft.

"It just looks that way Bub. Trust me on this."

"Trust you? That's not a very good idea Lee. Your ex says you're a liar," Bubba said as he landed the lens on moving forms coming down the campground road.

"My ex is the wicked beast of hell fire. And a lousy lay," I replied, my blood pressure soaring at the mention of Satan's daughter.

"Look Lee, there's Skeet and that blonde girl," Bubba said pointing at two flying figures running pell mell down the lane toting assorted clothing and Skeeter using his cap to cover his tiny privates.

"I think we better get in the car Bub, we may have to fly out of here," I said slipping into the driver's side and turning the key with a prayer.

"Yea, I see what you mean Lee. I think there's a man chasing them with a big stick."

"Just get in Bub and open the back door."

"All right,' Bubba said clunking into the front seat and unlatching the back door. With dust on their heels Mandy and Skeeter reached the car and threw their sweating bodies into the back and slammed the door shut.

"Drive! Drive damn it!" Skeeter blasted as Mandy struggled to put her bra on. I saw Mandy's breasts jiggling in the rear view mirror as I peeled the car onto the road and pushed the accelerator to the floorboard. We climbed to fifteen, then twenty miles an hour as a figure loomed in the rear window and heaved a stick at the car. It landed with a thud and broke out a taillight. Extraneous equipment, I thought, so I pushed the Pinto toward the Interstate and freedom from whatever it was that had chased us. Mandy dressed to my great disappointment. She had been quite a sight.

As the Pinto reached peak speed of sixty-five miles an hour I relaxed and pondered the predicament the two Luddites had acquired in the short period of an hour and fifteen minutes. Skeeter could get into trouble faster than a puppy in a glass shop. He is the most talented man I have ever known, though most of his talents are for undesirable activities. In a world that worshipped Pintos Skeeter would have been the most famous man alive, and I would have been his manager. We would have been rich and famous rather than piss poor and infamous. The world is a bitch on a stick that eats its young. Yet I would rather live on earth than anywhere else I have been.

"Look guys," I said after an hour, "The sun is almost down and we need to be somewhere for the night. I suggest we find a campground and make camp."

"Sure Lee," Bubba replied, "Camping sounds like fun, but can we roast marshmallows?"

"If we can find some, sure," I said hoping we would not.

"First one you see good buddy," Skeeter replied fondling Mandy's leg.

"Stop that Skeeter," Mandy giggled.

I rode the yellow beast along the Interstate of back woods Wyoming. Wyoming is the only place in America where the Interstate and a country road appear alike. I once heard a man say that there were more cows in Wyoming than people. But he was exaggerating; there are more squirrels in Wyoming than people. I saw a sign for Captain Jake's Camping Adventure and turned off the Interstate down a dirt road. Thick musky dust permeated the cabin and Bubba choked.

"Can't we just stay in a motel Lee?" The befuddled Bubba pleaded.

"Too late now, they're all full," I stated, though I just had no desire to spend money we did not have. I turned at the wooden sign and entered the 'ship-shapiest place on earth' according to the spray painted sign. A man in a sailor suit approached the window and for once I felt sorry for the working class.

"How many nights?" Little boy blue asked.

"Just one, be out at first light," I replied.

"Hemmingway said what is true is true at first light," the blue clad literature professor stated.

"Hemmingway blew his brains all over his hallway. Now, about a camp space," I responded, tired and dusty.

"You can take Pier twenty three over by the man made lake," Blue boy said taking a twenty-dollar bill out of my hand faster than a seagull after a fallen fry.

"Got it," I responded and pulled the old crate along the dry road toward space twenty-three. We arrived and I backed into the slender stall where a picnic table and a fire pit were the only clues of a campground. Bubba stretched his arms and exited the Pinto.

"This is fun Lee," Bubba stated.

"Uh-huh," I replied. The four of us pulled out the tiny tent and sleeping bags and Skeeter set to work putting the tent together. It was a three-man tent and there were four of us. Should be interesting, I thought. I walked up to the front and bought a bundle of firewood for ten dollars that looked like it had been picked up on the side of the road. However, it was dry. Bubba scrounged through the food bags for cans of chili and found four cans, but no opener. Skeeter took out his trusty hunting blade and opened the cans partway. I got a roaring blaze going and soon we had half heated cans of bad chili brewing on the grill. Bubba pined for marshmallows.

"Let's go back to the store Lee. I know they have some," Bubba whined.

"No way Bub, no can do. We have to save gas," I replied to a heartbroken and sullen Bubba.

Skeeter had the tent set and the bags stuffed in no time and the four of us sat haphazard about the roaring blaze as several neighbors snored in their RV's. I looked up and saw a plethora of stars, little suns spinning in the void against a backdrop of nothingness. I saw the edge of the Milky Way and thought it thick like a stream of icy milk from a spilled glass on my dresser. Billions of habitations lost forever to man because of distances too far for our limited minds to fathom. To think that aliens might have come from these far abodes to the little earth seemed preposterous, yet possible. Bubba looked up to yonder heavens through the miracle of super vision and thought he saw a triangular craft headed our way.

"Look everybody, a UFO," Bubba gleamed. I took a look and sure enough it was triangular. It was a slow moving vehicle sign stamped on the back of an ATV. I chuckled, but Bubba fretted.

"Sorry, Bub, that's just a sign," I said.

"Yea Lee, a sign of the apocalypse," Bubba replied.

"No Bub, literally a sign, like on the back of a slow moving vehicle," I stated as Skeeter and Mandy chuckled, "You need to look up at the sky and stay there."

"Oh."

No one could fault Bubba for his desire. He wanted more than anything for the world of aliens, Bigfoots, snow creatures, lake monsters, crop circles and buried treasure to be the one and true world, but so far the world had only been a disappointment of death and dust. Bubba cried out with his inner child for something miraculous to happen. And a miracle did happen, a neighbor came over and offered Bubba his left over marshmallows. Bubba was in momentary heaven thinking the world full of light and truth, beauty and love. It was a lot to ask of a white creamy confection.

"Oh shit," I exclaimed, "We didn't make our trip to the top today. We're going to have to really push it tomorrow. Maybe pull an all day hike."

"Wowzers Lee, that's a fur piece of hikin'," Skeeter stated as Mandy rubbed his leg.

"Yes sir, that it is," I replied looking into Mandy's eyes and seeing for the first time the lost little Mormon girl who had vanished under a mountain of football players and lost innocence. She had been raised with all the expectation imaginable. Marriage to a worthy priesthood holder, a temple wedding, sealing for time and eternity and a bundle of kids to keep her haggard and happy for decades to come. It had all vanished under a haze of temporal desecration. Mandy from Sandy was a slut. She could now speak of glory only in the past tense, her future as dim as the dust clouds of the Kuiper Belt. There is nothing so beautiful as the captured

remains of a lost and wondrous future, just look at the earth if you doubt
this truth.

"You know," I said babbling, "There are hundreds of billions of stars
out there. Some are earth like and some like Jupiter, but many worlds
capable of habitation. How can we be alone in all this vastness? How could
the universe be so frail as to produce just one planet teeming with life?

"Yes, that's what I've been saying Lee," Bubba exclaimed,
marshmallow on his cheek, "They're coming to contact us. I just know they
want to say hello."

"Or blow us all to hell," Skeeter replied.

"You know Joseph Smith said there are millions of inhabited worlds
out there. All of them filled with Heavenly Father's children," Mandy
stated, sounding odd and mysterious with her other world words.

"Man," Skeeter said, "That guy gets around."

"He has hundreds, maybe thousands of wives," Mandy said adjusting
her cumbersome bra.

"No wonder I can't get a girlfriend," Bubba replied, "They're all
taken."

The four of us sat and pondered the night sky as the fire dimmed to embers and then we all retired to the overwrought tent. Bubba was soon banished to the car for farting and I could not rest with Mandy and Skeeter humping like dogs trying to be quiet so as to not disturb me. I crawled out of the tent and slept under the multitude of white, twinkling lights that make up our galaxy. They whispered, winked and cried throughout the long night. God, I thought to myself, if there are thousands of inhabited worlds then somewhere up there is another loser just like me staring out at earth and wondering if intelligent life lives there. It is something I have been wondering myself.

Morning blasted over the low horizon and squirted yellow rays of sun into my rested eyeballs. The glory of the morning spread first to my eyes and then to all eyes as the sun rose inch by inch into the truth of the day. Perhaps Hemmingway was right, I thought, that what is true is true at first light. I arose and stood on a small bump of land just beyond the campground and saw God in the miracle of the morning. He was not the white bearded God of Skeeter's Sunday school or the paternal father of Mandy's primary days, but the boldness of time immemorial and the scintillating breathlessness of almost fourteen billion years of history. This was a God I could love and I thought for just a brief moment he was happy to see me standing on a bump of land realizing this plump, unambiguous truth. Perhaps this trip is not about seeing Wyoming, but about seeing life, I thought. I felt the breath of God over my shoulder.

"See Lee," Bubba said looking behind me through his super vision binoculars, "A crop circle right over there."

"I know Bub, I saw the craft that made it."

"You did?"

"It had a sign on the side that said 'earth or bust'."

"Oh my God Lee, wait 'til I tell all my friends about this," Bubba exclaimed like a kid discovering ice cream.

"I think you already did Bub," I replied as the sun bathed us in an envelope of whitewashed light and truth.

That day we climbed to the top of Devil's Tower, well Bubba only made it part way, and stared out at the vastness of America. It is a land of immense promise and possibility none of which had landed on the three of us. Only Mandy and her doe-eyed dreams had a chance for a future. We dropped her off at the Interstate rest area and Skeeter mourned all the way home. Along with Bubba pining for a UFO encounter it was not a fun ride.

Upon our return we all thought we had been changed by the experience, but we had just been made six days older. Truth is a rascal and pounces on us in the strangest of places, but those places are never of our choosing. Only truth knows where he is hiding and when he will strike. We humans must be patient and content if we are to ever know a damn thing. What I found at the Devil's Tower is the immensity of time and that, I believe, is greater than any spiritual enlightenment. Bubba and Skeeter agreed, though they were half asleep at the time. Perhaps all men are.

P. S. Yesterday the Air Force scrambled jets over Devil's Tower after air force security identified three oval shaped craft flying nearby. Bubba was in heaven.

FLORENCE HARPER

"I don't know sister, what we should do," Florence Harper said to her younger sister Nan.

"I think we should go on to Portland and get a motel for the night. I don't think this storm is going to let up," Nan replied, surveying the landscape with her pearl blue eyes. The red Chevy wagon slogged on, spraying water to either side of highway 99W. The rain was relentless, terrible even. Not that rain was unusual in Oregon in the middle of March, but that the length, depth and breadth of the rain had shut down the world of the Willamette Valley. Traveling from Albany to Seattle was a normal process in most cases, but the two sisters had started late and now had to decide if they would drive on to Seattle in the driving rain or stop for the night at a nearby motel along 99W. Florence, being the older, made the decision.

"We really need to get to Seattle if at all possible tonight sister," Florence stated.

"All right, but I just want it said that I thought the better of it," Nan replied.

"Duly noted. If you want I'll take over the driving sister," Florence offered.

"Yes, that would be nice," Nan replied. Nan searched for a convenient spot to pull over, but struggled to find just the right location. In 1967 the roads were not so well traveled and pullouts a rarity. Nan studied the edge of the highway for a place to pull over. They would be in Sherwood soon and there they could pull into a parking lot if need be. Nan put the wipers on high and leered into the glass in an attempt to see the road. If not for the white stripe she would not have been able to drive at all. The rain poured down in relentless fashion, pounding the road and the car in great dollops of moisture.

Spying a side road that appeared wide and easy Nan turned the Chevy off the highway onto the gravel drive that had sufficient turning radius to park and switch drivers and allow them back on the road. Florence said nothing as Nan took the car along the gravel edge looking for a safe spot to pull over. Florence spotted a circular driveway up ahead on a little knoll that would make their work light. Florence motioned for her sister to pull up to the drive by the wide gray house and Nan complied.

"It'll be easy to switch places up by the house and there's a big light on the shed so we can see," Florence stated.

"I see it sister, that's as good of a place as any," Nan replied. Nan drove steady through the driving rain toward the house humming a hymn she had sung last Sunday at the Baptist Church where she had been attending since a little girl in soft, silky dresses. Florence got out her black gloves she wore while driving in preparation for the long haul to Seattle that lay ahead. She thought of her mother, still alive and well, sitting home alone fretting over her two stubborn daughters that insisted on going out into the hard spring rain.

As the Chevy rose up over a small rise a deep ravine appeared to the left that was filled to capacity with the residue of several spring rains. It had been a wet spring so far and little of the current rain had flushed away as the ground and the drains were already over burdened.

"Watch out for that drop off sister," Florence commanded, "It looks terribly deep.

"I'm aware sis, I'll be careful."

Nan steered the car with infinite care as the road turned soft underneath the wheels. Jut then the road dipped and the back wheels slipped and sputtered in the rock and water base. Nan over steered to her right struggling to veer the car back on course, but the back passenger wheel slipped over the edge of the road and the car sagged onto the edge of the water filled basin. Nan gunned the accelerator in a vain attempt to right her course and the Chevy left the road as the two back wheels left contact with the road and the back of the car sagged into the water. The car slid backwards into the water.

"God have mercy!" Florence screamed into the black of the night.

"Roll down a window sis before we sink entirely," Nan exhorted.

Florence struggled to find the window roller in the dark as terror gripped her heart and thoughts of death entered her being. She missed and then missed again. He mind was filled with thousands of half thoughts collecting near where her judgment should be. Nan pushed on the car door as it sank deeper and deeper into the dank liquid. The pressure from the water intensified and she could not budge the door no matter how hard she tried.

"Start praying sis. Oh God hear me in my hour of need," Florence recited as panic claimed her sense and she tried again in vain to lower the window.

"We need to get a window down sis or we're going to drown!" Nan screamed.

Florence persisted in her efforts to no avail and Nan pushed and pulled at everything she could touch in a moment of panic so real it could be tasted on the tongue like rancid October apples. Moments turned into eternities as the car slid ever deeper and the light from above grew ever dimmer. At last Nan found the roller and freed herself from the car. She floated to the top to safety. Florence took in eight tiny gulps of water and released her will to God's. Nan ran to the house, but no one was home. The car lights faded in the black night and Florence Harper released the life in her body and stared into the darkness at the light overhead.

MAIN STREET

"Thank you ma'am, please come again," Blake said to the lady at the counter.

"Why thank you young man, but tell me why such a handsome fellow is still single?"

"Well Mrs. Cronin, I have no time. The mercantile keeps me plenty busy," Blake replied lifting the bag of groceries into a cart. He had bought the small grocery store in Tangent from Mr. Newman the month before and had been working twelve hours a day ever since. Blake loaded Mrs. Cronin up and she sped away in her Plymouth Fury.

Blake tidied behind the counter breathing in the autumn air that surrounded the store in suave self-assurance. As Blake stared out the window a young lady passed by on her way into the store. She sported red hair and freckles. He brushed his hair with his hand and returned to the counter to await the young lady with a touch of interest.

The young lady swept through the isles picking out fruit and eggs for her next day's breakfast. The basket full she crept up to the counter for tallying. Blake rang up the items on the cash register, which came to a total of $5.87. The young lady handed Blake six dollars. Her hands were soft like a whisper on a winter's day. He handed her the change and touched her hand. He loved the softness of her flesh against the rugged calluses of his own hands.

"I've never seen you here before," Blake said to the young woman.

"I just moved yesterday from Albany," she replied, "I have a sick grandmother over on third Street. I'm taking care of her now."

"I'm sorry to hear about your grandmother. I hope she's alright," Blake stated.

"She lost her second husband last month and I'm afraid she has a broken heart."

"Time heals most everything. I'm Blake Denney, proprietor," Blake said extending his hand.

"Molly Simmons." The two young people shook hands in the gentle manner of birds touching feathers then Molly noticed she had forgotten something. "Oh, I'm afraid I forgot to get some aspirin for my grandmother."

"I'll get it for you Molly." Blake leapt from behind the counter and discovered the aspirin on aisle three.

"Here you are Molly. No charge, consider it a gift to your grandmother's health," Blake said.

"Why that's very kind Mr. Denney. You don't need to….." Blake stopped her cold.

"My treat, now you have a wonderful night."

Molly smiled and lifted her bag from the counter leaving a small whiff of her perfume. As she reached the door she spun and smiled.

"Thank you again Mr. Denney," Molly said as her lithe legs moved her from the premises. She jaunted down Main Street. Blake breathed in her perfume and got a little dizzy. He returned to his work, but could not get the beautiful image of Molly Simmons from his mind. After an hour or so he leaned over to clean the bottom shelf of the produce isle when he was startled by a voice.

"Sorry to startle you Mr. Denney, but my grandmother was wondering if you might like to join us for dinner this evening. She thinks you aren't eating properly."

Blake rose to his full height of six feet and stared into the green eyes of the young woman.

"I would be delighted," Blake said with a big grin.

"Seven thirty, fourth house on the right after you pass Main Street onto Third. We're having stew and biscuits. I hope that's all right," Molly stated.

"More than all right. I'll bring a bottle of wine from my stock."

"Excellent. I'll see you then Mr. Denney."

Molly exited, proper and prompt, but Blake could also see a sensual quality in the lady. Blake worked until six-thirty and hurried to his apartment to clean up.

Blake dressed in his best suit and tie and manicured his hair in the small mirror in the bathroom. He wanted to look his best for Molly. He had a feeling about her, that she just might be a big part of his future, a future that up to that afternoon had not existed. He walked up the three and a half blocks to Molly's grandmother's house and knocked on the door, a bottle of good vintage under his arm. Molly answered the door frocked in a red dress that flattered her figure. He almost gasped.

"Come in Mr. Denney," Molly offered. She motioned him to the sofa by the dining room where grandmother sat in her rocker, shawl draped over her shoulders for warmth.

"Hello," Blake said, having the dubious distinction of not knowing the grandmother's name.

"So," Grandmother began, "You're my date. That's good, I like 'em young."

Blake laughed and in that instant Molly knew she had met a man of quality. Molly motioned for Blake to yield the bottle of wine and the three of them soon toasted to good health.

After supper Blake had to beg his leave as five A.M. came early. As he stood in the doorway Molly slipped up next to him and gave him a peck on the cheek. He blushed.

"Thank you for coming, grandmother enjoyed it very much, you are such a dear. She laughed at all your jokes."

"I had a delightful time," Blake replied staring into Molly's eyes, "Perhaps next time you and I could go out on a date."

"I'd love that," Molly replied.

In the cool of the morning Blake was hard at work when a flushed Molly Simmons came pouring through the front door.

"Oh Blake," she began, "I'm afraid grandmother has taken ill. She went to bed last night and woke up feverish."

"That's terrible Molly. Is there anything I can do?"

"Just hold me. I have no one."

"Me either," Blake responded gliding the gentle girl into his arms. Out on Main Street passersby looked inside in disgust, assuming that impropriety had entered the sanctuary of their quiet town.

GRANDMA GRIMM GETS A GIMP

Grandma Grimm, a snuff-sniffing ball of seventy-five year old lightening, was my favorite grandmother of the six women that I called by that name over the years. She was not my real grandmother, but she was old and that she also slept with my still frisky seventy-seven year old grandfather made her qualify for the title by deed if not by seed. She did everything a person should not do and that made her captivating to a boy of six. The first time I saw her she was sitting in the front yard made of pine needles and dirt drinking iced tea out of an old mason jar and spitting homilies into the Oregon wind. She blasted her words into air so thick you could slice it with a chainsaw, which she did many times.

From her soapbox, and I mean just that, she dispensed her Okie wisdom with the demeanor and inquisitiveness of a wrinkled Socrates. Little she said stuck with me through the years, most of it pure bullshit anyway, but the way she flowered her words has influenced the way I speak today and why I am the most sought after public speaker in Priggy County. I am counted on to give graduation speeches at the kindergarten and to open the go-cart speedway every year as well as participate in the pig calling contest at the county fair between sips of home brew. Grandma Grimm was my inspiration and I still see her today in my mind's eye standing up with her one withered leg and pounding the ground with her cane and shaking her head with vigor after a good snort of snuff. She swilled iced tea between tirades to keep her energy up. Grandma Grimm had enormous energy for a woman who never did a damn thing.

One day she told the story of how she got her gimp. I had been sent out to the farm in August to allow my parents to go to Vegas to win my college education fund. Grandma Grimm sat out on her soapbox in the heat of the August evening, surrounded by her three grandkids from her previous eight marriages and several of my little cousins and started to speak. The concourse grew whisper quiet as if Moses were about to speak.

Grandma put a tin of snuff to her tobacco-colored tongue and tilted her head back and then shook her neck for all she was worth. It looked something like what a holy roller looks like after a come to Jesus meeting. This is what I think she said.

"It was a fine day, sun out, frogs hoppin' and crickets rubbin'. I was only twelve year old and I was the fastest runner in the entire world. My cousin Jake thought he was faster, but he wasn't. I was. So we lined up near the side of a deep ditch and commenced to run as fast as our little legs would carry us. I pounded and pounded my legs into the soft earth, but little Jake was gaining on me. We were almost to the chicken coop, where our race was to end, and he had a good step on me so I flung my little body into his and I knocked him to the ground and stepped over the finish line first. He was not too amused so he picked me up and threw me into the ditch. There was a big pump there for pulling irrigation water out of the channel and my leg got stuck in it. Jake hollered and hollered until help arrived and they wanted to saw my leg off, but I wouldn't let 'em. I screamed bloody murder and yanked and yanked on my leg until I heard everythin' pop and snap like sapless limbs from a burlywood tree. I dragged myself to shore and laid there, my leg torn to pieces and then my uncle and father said they had only been foolin', they weren't goin' to cut my leg off at all. When they saw I had busted my leg they laughed. I spit on my uncle and headed down the dirt road toward town and married the first man I met. He was ugly as sin and had a bobble-butt for a nose. I loathed him, but he loved my gimpy leg 'cause he knew I wouldn't run off. I didn't have to. Two years later I killed him in his sleep with a baseball bat and said a robber had done it. I was fourteen when I left there with my gimp. Now none of this is true, mind you, if the police should come out askin' questions."

Grandma Grimm stopped speaking and looked down at her enthralled audience. I was flushed with disbelief, but my little cousins believed every word. I think this is part of the reason they are today in Arizona looking for the meaning of life at the High Holiness Temple of the Rising Stocks and RV park. My cousin Sally Sue asked me if I wanted to race. I declined. Grandma Grimm sat back down on her soapbox and swilled a large offering of iced tea. She looked out over the horizon and said, "Tomorrow I'll tell ya all how I got the habit of snuff from my grandfather Bud." Now that was a story I wanted to hear. Grandma Grimm died years later crossing Elm Street on her way to the liquor store, those that said she would die from snorting snuff were proven dead wrong.

TWO RIVERS, ONE SOUL

"Do you think the world will remember us Henry?" Donna Wright asked in the cool of the evening.

"No. A few friends and family, not many other than that," Henry Rollins answered. The chill of the evening swept over the couple sitting side by side on a wooden bench overlooking the intersection of two rivers, the swift Willamette and the languid Metolius.

"It seems sad, not to be remembered," Donna said as a leaf departed a nearby maple and tumbled to the ground.

"No one is remembered for long, perhaps a few thousand years at best and then oblivion. The world is constantly covering the past with layers of silt."

"I suppose you're right, but it still seems sad. Let's toast to the future, however short and bleak it may be," Donna said raising a wine glass full of Cabernet. Henry raised his glass to meet hers and the two lovers clanged glasses and drank the red liquid until it was gone.

"I should be getting you back. Your mother will be worried if you're out past dark," Henry said lamenting the fact that Donna, twenty-two years old, still lived with her sickly mother.

"I don't want to go back to my house. Let's walk back to your apartment love," Donna said then looked away at the fading light of the September day.

"Are you sure?" Henry quizzed, uncertain he had heard the beautiful girl correctly.

"Yes, I'm sure."

Henry raised his lanky body and held out his hand to be taken. Donna accepted his hand and the two young lovers strolled down the boardwalk toward Henry's upstairs apartment behind Smith's clothing store on First Street.

"Are you sure we shouldn't stop by your mother's and let her know where you are?" Henry asked, concerned that the police might be at his door before morning.

"Actually Henry, I told her before I left that I wouldn't be home until morning," Donna said smiling toward her feet.

"You are full of surprises my dear."

Henry stepped quick and sure down the boardwalk etched along the banks of the Willamette River. They passed store after store, all closed, until at last they reached Henry's apartment door and the two lovers walked up the stairs and entered Henry's flat.

"It's quite a bachelor's apartment Henry dear. But I expected as much," Donna said laying her shawl on the banister by the living room.

"Well I work a lot of hours, not much time for cleaning and decorating. It could use a woman's touch I'm afraid."

"That it could," Donna said wishing she were that woman.

"Please, take a seat my love," Henry said pointing to the sofa by the picture window. Donna sat down, tucking her dress underneath her.

"You have quite a view Henry. You can see the river from your picture window. I would never have guessed you possessed such luxurious accommodations."

"Yes well, it's just a happenstance I'm afraid. The apartment just happens to be next to the river and I have a window," Henry said taking a seat next to his girlfriend of six months. He was twenty-six and had taken the virtue of seven young maidens in Albany, but never so delicious a prize as the daughter of a former judge, may he rest in peace. He loved Donna, but not in the way she supposed. He loved the idea of her more than her living flesh and blood. He was in love with the prospects a girl with such connections would bring him. He leaned over and kissed her.

"My you're very forward tonight," Donna said in mocking fashion, knowing her consent to be in his apartment implied far more.

"I love you Donna, with all my heart."

Donna blushed and then said, "And I you."

Henry kissed Donna again and then placed his hand under her cheek.

"I've never shown you the entire apartment," Henry said knowing the only room not seen from their vantage point was the bedroom and a small bathroom in the hall.

"Well we can't have a girl ignorant of her lover's apartment now can we?"

"Absolutely not," Henry said and then stood up, catching a glimpse of the two rivers out his window as he looked up.

"What a view Henry. Who would have guessed?"

Henry escorted his lover to his bedroom where he closed the door with a measure of authority.

"I've never done this Henry, with anyone," Donna said hoping that her confession would ensure Henry's gentleness.

"I know dear. I am a gentle man and a gentleman."

Donna smiled and then walked into Henry's arms. He wrapped his arms around her small torso and they embraced with the tightness of newlyweds. Donna knew she would not be Henry's first, but she did not want to know an exact number. Henry's past was to her only a shadow in a mist.

Henry laid the girl down on his bed and looked at her for a long minute before removing his shirt. Donna unbuttoned her blouse and Henry removed her blouse and bra with cautious determination. Before long the two lovers lie side by side naked and aroused. Henry claimed his prize and the night wore on as he two spent lovers rested.

In the morning a robin flitted on a branch outside Henry's window. He awoke to the sound of almost nothing and realized that he had changed everything with his actions of the night before. He knew that Donna now expected a proposal of marriage in the near future. Henry didn't know if he was ready for such commitment. He strained to awaken in the rising dawn and collected his clothes and his thoughts before making his way to the bathroom down the narrow hallway.

He dressed and went into the tiny kitchen to make breakfast and to put on a pot of coffee. He could hear Donna stirring in the bedroom and he rued the awkwardness of their first morning together.

"Good morning love," Donna said as she entered the kitchen wrapped in a long shirt borrowed from Henry.

"Aren't you a sight first thing in the morning. And that shirt fits you perfectly."

"Thank you sir," Donna said taking a seat on the metal chair beside the kitchen table.

"Care for some coffee?" Henry asked.

"Yes, that would be wonderful," Donna said, rubbing her eyes from the strain of a half night of sleep.

Henry poured a cup of coffee for the adorable girl at his table.

"Will you marry me?" Henry blurted before he could censure his words.

"No."

"No?"

"Why buy the cow when you can get the milk for free?" Donna said before laughing out loud.

"I thought that was a man's line?" Henry said before he too burst out laughing, "So that's really a yes?"

"Yes," Donna said then leapt out of the chair to embrace her lover.

"What a strange thing a life is," Henry said to the wall, but Donna did not hear him.